NORTH AMERICAN DINOSAURS

HADROSAURUS

ANASTASIA SUEN

Rourke Educational Media
A Division of Carson Dellosa Education
rourkeeducationalmedia.com

ROURKE'S
SCHOOL to HOME
CONNECTIONS

BEFORE AND DURING READING ACTIVITIES

Before Reading: *Building Background Knowledge and Vocabulary*

Building background knowledge can help children process new information and build upon what they already know. Before reading a book, it is important to tap into what children already know about the topic. This will help them develop their vocabulary and increase their reading comprehension.

Questions and Activities to Build Background Knowledge:

1. Look at the front cover of the book and read the title. What do you think this book will be about?
2. What do you already know about this topic?
3. Take a book walk and skim the pages. Look at the table of contents, photographs, captions, and bold words. Did these text features give you any information or predictions about what you will read in this book?

Vocabulary: *Vocabulary Is Key to Reading Comprehension*

Use the following directions to prompt a conversation about each word.

- Read the vocabulary words.
- What comes to mind when you see each word?
- What do you think each word means?

Vocabulary Words:

- *asteroid*
- *bill*
- *conifers*
- *crest*
- *Deinosuchus*
- *fossil*
- *grazing*
- *herd*
- *iguana*
- *vandals*

During Reading: *Reading for Meaning and Understanding*

To achieve deep comprehension of a book, children are encouraged to use close reading strategies. During reading, it is important to have children stop and make connections. These connections result in deeper analysis and understanding of a book.

Close Reading a Text

During reading, have children stop and talk about the following:

- Any confusing parts
- Any unknown words
- Text to text, text to self, text to world connections
- The main idea in each chapter or heading

Encourage children to use context clues to determine the meaning of any unknown words. These strategies will help children learn to analyze the text more thoroughly as they read.

When you are finished reading this book, turn to the next-to-last page for **Text-Dependent Questions** and an **Extension Activity**.

TABLE OF CONTENTS

FINDING *HADROSAURUS*

A dinnertime story led to the discovery of a dinosaur! William Parker Foulke was on vacation. His friend John Hopkins invited him to come over for dinner. At dinner, someone started talking about some strange old bones. Twenty years earlier, workers had found them in the marl behind Hopkins's New Jersey home.

Marl is clay with calcium in it. Farmers used marl as fertilizer. Why were there large bones in it? Foulke wanted to know more. But Hopkins had given all of the old bones away. They had been gone for 20 years. Foulke asked if he could dig for more bones. Hopkins agreed.

The marl pit where the bones were found in New Jersey is now a United States National Historic Landmark.

Dr. Joseph Leidy (1823–1891) was the founder of American vertebrate paleontology.

It took two days of digging to find the old marl pit. Ten feet (three meters) down, the diggers found more large bones. It was the left side of a massive creature! They found a hip, a front leg, back legs, and nine teeth. They also dug up 28 vertebrae, the creature's backbones.

Foulke notified Dr. Joseph Leidy. He was a professor at the University of Pennsylvania. He knew all about old creatures with backbones. The professor came out to the farm. The workers kept digging for months, but they didn't find any more bones.

Illustrations of Hadrosaurus *bones from Joseph Leidy's 1865 book* Cretaceous Reptiles of the United States

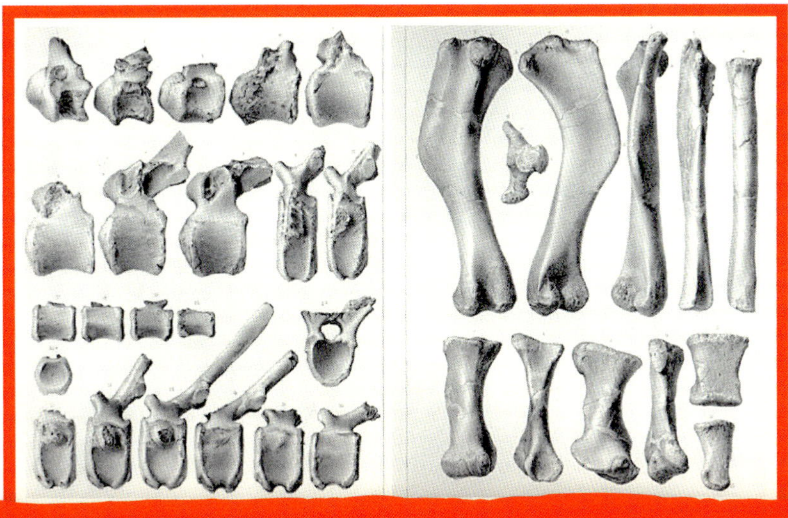

Bulky Lizard

The professor gave the creature a name. He called it "bulky lizard" in Greek. He added Foulke's name too. The new dinosaur's name was *Hadrosaurus foulkii*.

WOODEN BOXES

After the bones were dug up, they were placed in wooden boxes. Wagons carried them for 12 miles (19 kilometers) to Philadelphia. The bones were sent to the Academy of Natural Sciences.

That *Hadrosaurus* found in 1858 was a first. Until that time, other **fossil** hunters had found only teeth and small bones. No one had ever found so much of one dinosaur before. The bones in the marl pit in New Jersey were the first big fossil find. News spread around the world. Everyone wanted to see them.

A CHORUS OF COLORS
FROGS
FEB.4–MAY 14
ansp.org
A CHORUS OF COLORS
FROGS
FEB.4–MAY 14
ansp.org
THE ACADEMY OF NATURAL SCIENCES OF PHILADELPHIA
MUSEUM
NO STOPPING
ANY TIME
ONLY
ONLY
APRIL 1-2
THE ACADEMY
OF NATURAL SCIENCES
THE ACADEMY
OF NATURAL SCIENCES

The Crystal Palace models were constructed in Hawkins's studio near the park.

Benjamin Waterhouse (B.W.) Hawkins wanted to see the bones. He was a sculptor. Hawkins had built a large dinosaur exhibit in London. The dinosaur models in Crystal Palace Park were life-sized.

Hawkins wanted to make another dinosaur exhibit in New York. He asked the Academy of Natural Sciences if he could make a copy of the *Hadrosaurus*. If they let him copy it, he would make one for the academy too. They agreed.

Hawkins used models of the bones to make two life-sized *Hadrosaurus* mounts. In 1868, the academy put their *Hadrosaurus* on display. People came from all over to see it. It was the first dinosaur exhibit in the United States.

Safe!

Using models of the bones turned out to be a good idea. The *Hadrosaurus* model in New York was destroyed by **vandals**. The bones were safe inside their wooden boxes at the academy. They are still there today.

THE MISSING HEAD

The workers in New Jersey didn't find a complete skull in the marl. So Hawkins improvised. He made a model of an **iguana** head for his models.

In the years that followed, fossil hunters found more bones. They studied the bones and looked for clues. This is the science of paleontology.

How do they figure out what they dug up? Scientists look at the clues. They make notes about how far down they had to dig. They bring the bones back and study them.

IGUANA

Hadrosaurs

The head of the first "bulky lizard" was never found, but that didn't stop scientists. They looked at the bones they had and soon discovered more bones like them. This new group of dinosaurs was named *hadrosaurs*.

The heads of the hadrosaurs scientists found had different shapes. Some had a long, low head. Others had a head with a huge bump on top.

The bump looked like a helmet, but it was made of bone. The bump is called a **crest**. The crest was hollow or empty inside. New models of *Hadrosaurus* have a crest.

A hollow crest might have helped it make sounds. It might have sounded like a trumpet. It might have sounded like a horn. The sounds may have warned of danger. They may have been a call to a mate.

LAMBEOSAURUS

PARASAUROLOPHUS

EDMONTOSAURUS

All of the skulls, bumpy or flat, looked the same in the front. All of them had a long **bill** like a duck. This gave the hadrosaurs another name. They are also called duck-billed dinosaurs.

Like a duck, a hadrosaur was an herbivore. This gentle giant only ate plants. It lived in forests and swamps where pine trees and other **conifers** grew.

A hadrosaur ripped needles, twigs, and seeds from the trees with its bill. It ground up the tough plant parts with hundreds of teeth. When the teeth wore out, new ones popped up to take their place.

STANDING UP

At first, Professor Leidy thought that this dinosaur stood up like a kangaroo. The front leg bones were much shorter than the back leg bones. When Hawkins made the models, he used the kangaroo pose. When he stood next to this model, his head reached the dinosaur's knee.

After other hadrosaurs were found, the model was changed. Old footprints in the mud had turned into fossils. After millions of years, they had turned into stone. These fossil footprints told a different story. The long tail didn't drag on the ground. It was up in the air for balance. The long, stiff tail helped keep *Hadrosaurus* from tipping over.

FOSSILIZED HADROSAUR
SKIN IMPRESSION (CAST)

Hadrosaurus was a slow mover. It walked on all four legs when it was **grazing**. It only walked on its back legs when it had to run.

Hundreds of huge bodies moved and swayed together. *Hadrosaurus* was a **herd** animal. The herd lumbered slowly from place to place looking for food.

Duck-billed dinosaurs were not good at fighting. They did not have sharp teeth. They did not have big claws. But they probably had good eyesight and hearing to help them avoid their enemies.

Terror Crocodile

A monster reptile slithered through the swamps and rivers. It was ***Deinosuchus***, which means "terror crocodile." Its tube-shaped body stretched 36 feet (11 meters). It was three feet (one meter) longer than the *Hadrosaurus* it hunted. Its massive jaws were spiked with razor-sharp teeth. Run!

Hadrosaurus herds stopped to raise babies. These dinosaurs laid eggs in nests. The babies pecked their way out of the shells. Mothers took care of the babies.

The babies were small. They were about 14 inches (36 centimeters) long. They weighed about one pound (454 grams). The babies grew to be about 30 feet (nine meters) long. That's as long as a school bus.

Bumpy

All hadrosaurs had leathery skin covering their bodies. Bumps stuck up from the tough skin. The bumps may have held feathers. Did *Hadrosaurus* have brightly colored feathers? Scientists don't know.

EXTINCT!

Finding the first *Hadrosaurus* led to the discovery of many types of hadrosaurs. They all lived in a time called the Cretaceous Period. There were more hadrosaurs than any other kind of dinosaur. They were called "the cows of the Cretaceous."

Earth was warm and wet when *Hadrosaurus* was alive. Forests and swamps covered much of the land. There were many trees and flowers. All kinds of insects buzzed around.

Hadrosaurs

AMUROSAURUS

BRACHYLOPHOSAURUS

LAMBEOSAURUS

OURANOSAURUS

PARASAUROLOPHUS

SAUROLOPHUS

SHANTUNGOSAURUS

VELAFRONS

About 65 million years ago, *Hadrosaurus* disappeared. Many scientists think that an **asteroid** slammed into Earth. The damage it caused could be the reason that these dinosaurs became extinct. It may have caused smoke and ash to cover the planet. That would have blocked the sunlight. Without sunlight, the plants couldn't grow. This meant *Hadrosaurus* wouldn't have anything to eat. Without food, it would die.

State Dinosaur

States in the United States have official flags. Many states have an official state flower or state bird. New Jersey has a state dinosaur. It is the *Hadrosaurus*! It was discovered near Haddonfield. Schoolchildren in that town helped make it the state dinosaur. They helped get a law passed in 1991 that made *Hadrosaurus* the official dinosaur of New Jersey.

Where to Hunt Dinosaurs

Hadrosaurus foulkii was found in Haddonfield, New Jersey. Other hadrosaurs have been found across North America. They have also been found in South America, Europe, and Asia.

Time Line: *Hadrosaurus* and You

Do you see yourself on the time line? Look at the far right. You live in the Quaternary Period of the Cenozoic Era. Dinosaurs lived in the era before ours. They roamed Earth in the Mesozoic Era.

The Mesozoic Era had three time periods. *Hadrosaurus* lived in the last one. They were Cretaceous dinosaurs. They lived on Earth 145 to 65 million years ago.

Hadrosaurus
145–65 million years ago

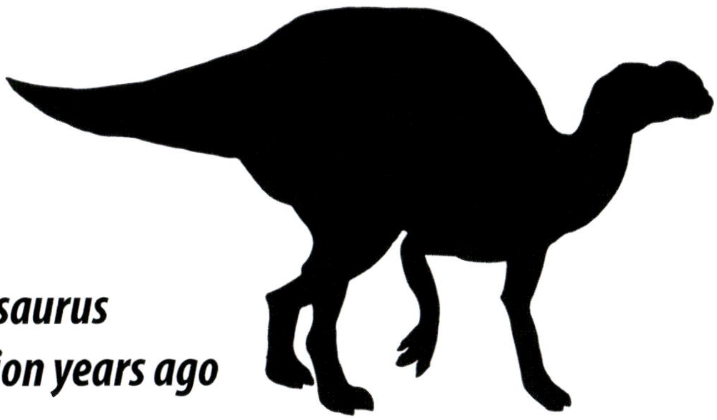

YOU!

MESOZOIC			CENOZOIC	
Triassic	Jurassic	Cretaceous	Tertiary	Quaternary
251–199.6 million years ago	199.6–145.5 million years ago	145.5–65.5 million years ago	65.5–1.81 million years ago	1.81–NOW million years ago

GLOSSARY

asteroid (AS-tuh-roid): a rock in space

bill (bil): the jaws and beak of a bird or other animal

conifers (KAH-nuh-furs): evergreen trees with needle-shaped leaves and cones

crest (krest): a lump on the head of an animal

Deinosuchus (DIE-no-SOO-kuss): a large crocodile that is now extinct

fossil (FAH-suhl): a plant or animal part from long ago that has turned into a rock

grazing (GRAY-zing): feeding on grasses and low-lying plants

herd (hurd): a group of animals that live and move together

iguana (i-GWAH-nuh): a large lizard that lives in warm places

vandals (VAN-duhls): people who damage or destroy things on purpose

INDEX

TEXT-DEPENDENT QUESTIONS

1. Why was the professor notified after the bones were found?
2. How did using a model protect the bones?
3. Explain why this massive dinosaur is compared to a small bird that swims in the water.
4. What did the fossil footprints show about this dinosaur?
5. What might have happened when this dinosaur saw a *Deinosuchus* in the swamp?

EXTENSION ACTIVITY

Practice your paleontology skills! Use air-dry clay to make your own model of a *Hadrosaurus* head. Will you give it a large or a small crest? Or do you think it should have a long, low head? Explain your reasons.

ABOUT THE AUTHOR

Anastasia Suen is the author of more than 300 books for young readers. Her children were both dinosaur fans, so she took them to the Natural History Museum of Los Angeles County and the La Brea Tar Pits often. They called both of these sites the "dinosaur" museum!

www.rourkeeducationalmedia.com

PHOTO CREDITS: Cover and Title page ©Joe Tucciarone; Pg 4 ©Smallbones @ Wiki; Pg 5 ©François Gohier; Pg 6 ©Gilbert Studios; Pg 7 ©Leidy @ Wiki; Pg 8 ©Pi-Lens; Pg 9 ©4kclips; Pg 10 ©Philip Henry Delamotte; Pg 11 ©Lucas, Frederic Augustus @ Wiki; Pg 12 ©zlato; Pg 13, 23 ©François Gohier; Pg 14 ©Zissoudisctrucker @ Wiki; Pg 15, 19 ©Jim, the Photographer @ Wiki; Pg 16 ©Reimar, Dinoton, Pimpay; Pg 17 ©Jan Sovak; Pg 18 ©Michael Vigliotti; Pg 20 ©CoreyFord; Pg 21 ©Picasa; Pg 22 ©Davide Bonadonna; OllgaP; Pg 24 ©Daniel Eskridge; Pg 25 ©Debivort @ Wiki; Pg 25©Warpaintcobra, CoreyFord, Xialmages, Elenarts; Pg 26 ©adventtr; Pg 28, 29 ©ONYXprj; Pg 29 ©ChrisGorgio

Edited by: Kim Thompson
Cover design by: Rhea Magaro-Wallace
Interior design by: Janine Fisher

Library of Congress PCN Data

Hadrosaurus / Anastasia Suen
(North American Dinosaurs)
ISBN 978-1-73161-449-0 (hard cover)
ISBN 978-1-73161-244-1 (soft cover)
ISBN 978-1-73161-554-1 (e-Book)
ISBN 978-1-73161-659-3 (ePub)
Library of Congress Control Number: 2019932149

Rourke Educational Media
Printed in the United States of America,
North Mankato, Minnesota